W9-BQZ-985

A Junior Novelization

Adapted by Daniela Burr

Based on the original screenplay
by Cliff Ruby & Elana Lesser

SCHOLASTIC INC.

New York   Toronto   London   Auckland   Sydney
Mexico City   New Delhi   Hong Kong   Buenos Aires

If you purchased this book without a cover, you should be aware that this book is stolen property. It was reported as "unsold and destroyed" to the publisher, and neither the author nor the publisher has received any payment for this "stripped book."

No part of this publication may be reproduced in whole or part, stored in a retrieval system, or transmitted in any form or by any means, electronic, mechanical, photocopying, recording, or otherwise, without written permission of the copyright owner. For information regarding permission, write to Scholastic Inc., Attention: Permissions Department, 557 Broadway, New York, NY 10012.

ISBN 0-439-87003-8

BARBIE and associated trademarks and trade dress are owned by, and used under license from, Mattel, Inc. © 2006 Mattel, Inc. All Rights Reserved.

Special thanks to Vicki Jaeger, Monica Okazaki, Rob Hudnut, Shelley Dvi-Vardhana, Jesyca C. Durchin, Shea Wageman, Jennifer Twiner McCarron, Trevor Wyatt, Greg Richardson, Derek Goodfellow, Genevieve Lacombe, Theresa Johnston, Michael Douglas, David Pereira, Jonathon Busby, Sean Newton, Zoe Evamy, Steve Lumley, and Walter P. Martishius.

Published by Scholastic Inc.
SCHOLASTIC and associated logos are trademarks and/or registered trademarks of Scholastic Inc.

12 11 10 9 8 7 6 5 4 3 2 1   6 7 8 9 10/0

Printed in the U.S.A.
First printing, August 2006

Chapter 1
Princesses at Play

There once lived a kind, understanding king and his twelve beautiful daughters. The princesses were known far and wide for the grace they displayed whenever they twirled in beautiful pirouettes across the countryside. In fact, they were often called the Twelve Dancing Princesses.

As King Randolph's daughters became older, it was expected that they would begin to attend royal galas and dinners in other lands. It was for that very reason that the ambassador from Bulovia had requested an audience with King Randolph.

The king yawned as the Bulovian ambassador unfurled a long scroll. In a very official voice, the ambassador cleared his throat and announced, "I am authorized by my courageous king and beautiful queen to hereby invite the princesses of King Randolph to a royal gala —"

Before he could read another word, three young princesses came racing into the throne room.

"Papa, Papa, look what I found!" Princess Janessa shouted, obviously not noticing that her father was entertaining company.

"You won't believe it," Princess Kathleen added.

"Janessa, Kathleen, wait for me!" Lacey, the smallest of the triplets, shouted as she struggled to catch up to her sisters.

The ambassador looked at the girls with

surprise, then tried to continue reading from his scroll. "As I was saying —" he began.

"It's a blue-winged beetle," Janessa continued excitedly, ignoring the ambassador. She opened her cupped hands and shoved the beetle under her father's nose. "It makes a strange noise when it . . ."

Before Janessa could finish her sentence, the beetle flew off. It circled around the king's head and then made its way toward the ambassador.

The ambassador opened his mouth to speak, but he was cut off by the sound of a croquet ball rolling through the throne room. It was followed by Princess Edeline and Princess Delia, both carrying croquet mallets.

"Playing through," Edeline called out. "We'll just be a second, Papa."

Delia hit the ball with her mallet. It bounced off a chair and narrowly missed King

Randolph's head. "Sorry," Delia apologized. "Too much wrist."

The Bulovian ambassador turned up his nose as the girls left the room. "Are the others like these?" the ambassador asked.

As if to answer him, two more princesses — the twins, Hadley and Isla — stomped into the throne room on stilts.

"Look, Papa, we can make it . . ." Isla began.

"All the way to the door," Hadley finished her thought.

Isla took another step. "Whoa," she cried out as she began to topple over. In a moment, the stilts collapsed beneath her. As Isla fell, she knocked into Hadley, and both the twins fell to the ground in a giggling heap.

The ambassador could take no more. "Perhaps another ball, Your Highness," he told the king. "These girls would be the laughingstock of the gala."

King Randolph sighed heavily. If only Queen Isabella were here to help him. But, sadly, the princesses' mother had died years before. Still, something had to be done to tame the princesses' behavior. He would speak to them about it at lunch.

Later that day, the king and his daughters

gathered in the royal dining room. As the king took his seat, he looked around the table at his beautiful offspring: the two eldest girls, Ashlyn and Blair, who greeted him with a kiss; Courtney, who, as usual, could not pull her nose from her book long enough to eat a meal; Delia and Edeline, the sportswomen; Fallon, the romantic; the playful twins, Hadley and Isla; and, of course, the endlessly energetic triplets, Janessa, Kathleen, and Lacey.

But one princess was missing.

"Hmmm . . . where is Genevieve?" the king murmured to himself. He did not sound at all surprised that his sixteen-year-old daughter was late for lunch, again.

At just that moment, a furry little head popped up from the empty seat at the table. A moment later, the rest of the furry body leaped onto the table. Twyla, Princess Genevieve's playful kitten, had arrived.

"Twyla, off the table," the king demanded.

Just then, Twyla's mistress, the beautiful Princess Genevieve, burst into the room. "Sorry I'm late, Papa," she apologized.

The king smiled at his beautiful, blond daughter and cleared his throat. "Quiet, please," he asked his daughters as he prepared to speak to them about their behavior.

Unfortunately, the king never had the chance to speak to his daughters. No sooner did the girls quiet down than the royal butler announced that Derek, the royal cobbler, had arrived with a chest of brand-new shoes for the girls.

And not just any shoes.

Dancing shoes!

The princesses could not resist those! They nearly flew to see the treasures Derek had brought them.

The king was left alone in the dining room

with Twyla. And there was nothing he could do but shake his head in frustration and say, "*Bon appétit*, Twyla," as they both began eating their soup.

Chapter 2
Dancing Shoes

As the princesses spilled into the garden, Derek's eyes fell on Princess Genevieve. She was by far the most beautiful of the girls, with her long, flowing blond hair and wide blue eyes. The cobbler sighed heavily at the sight of her.

"I love the colors!" Princess Delia exclaimed, shaking Derek from his thoughts.

"You're amazing, Derek," Princess Ashlyn added as she took a long look at the chest of dancing shoes.

Derek blushed slightly at the compliments. "I — I'm glad they meet with your approval, Highnesses."

Suddenly, a colorful bird fluttered through the sky and landed on Derek's shoulder. "I taught him everything he knows," the bird squawked.

After all of her sisters had chosen their shoes, Genevieve approached the cobbler. "Anything for me?" she asked Derek shyly.

"He burned the midnight oil for *you*," Felix cawed.

Genevieve's eyes flew open, and she looked at Derek with surprise. Derek blushed and shooed the bird from his shoulder.

"He . . . he's just a bird. . . ." the cobbler murmured. "He . . . uh . . . doesn't know what he's saying."

Genevieve's face fell slightly. "Of course,"

she replied, trying hard not to let her disappointment show.

Derek shyly handed Genevieve a beautifully wrapped package. "These are yours," he said quietly. "I hope you like them, Your Highness."

Before Genevieve could even open the package, the twins, Hadley and Isla, raced over and grabbed Derek by the arm. "Could you please . . ." Hadley began. "Tighten our shoes," Isla finished her sentence.

And with that, Derek was gone, leaving Genevieve all by herself.

"You blew your chance, Romeo," Felix

cawed into Derek's ear as the cobbler finished fastening the twins' shoes.

"What chance?" Derek sighed ruefully. "I'm just a cobbler. She doesn't even notice me." He looked over in Genevieve's direction. The princess had already placed the rosy pink satin dancing shoes on her feet and was dancing across the lawn. The late evening sunlight framed her gentle face, and her blond hair billowed behind her in the breeze as she moved. She looked like an angel.

"All we're missing is music," Princess Delia said as she leaped up to join her sister.

"Music?" Felix asked. He reached down with his beak and pulled a small pennywhistle from Derek's pocket.

"Hey," Derek cried out, trying to grab the whistle from his bird.

"Will you play for us?" Janessa asked.

"As you wish, Your Highnesses," Derek

said shyly. He placed the tiny flute between his lips and began to play. The Twelve Dancing Princesses twirled with joy.

King Randolph watched from the throne room window as the girls danced. He knew his daughters needed guidance to turn them into proper princesses, but he didn't know the first thing about how to guide them. He looked up at the portrait of his late wife.

"If only you were here," he said sadly.

Chapter 3
The Duchess Arrives

One week after the ambassador's ill-fated appointment, another visitor arrived at the castle. This time it was Duchess Rowena, King Randolph's cousin.

Rowena loved being a member of the royal family. She enjoyed nothing more than bossing people around — particularly her manservant, Desmond.

"Welcome, Duchess Rowena," the royal butler greeted her. "The king has been expecting you."

Suddenly, a small brown monkey scampered to the doorway and promptly planted himself at Rowena's feet.

"Heavens!" the royal butler exclaimed. "What is it?"

"My pet monkey, Brutus," Rowena told him. "Don't tell me the king doesn't have one. They're all the rage."

The butler didn't reply. He merely led Rowena and her monkey into the Great Hall and went off in search of the king. Once she was left on her own, Rowena began studying the various items in the Great Hall. She fingered an elaborately embroidered brocade tablecloth and smiled greedily. "Hmm. Very nice," she murmured. Then she picked up a small box and took a good long look at her reflection in the shiny silver. "Perfect," she complimented herself.

When she heard footsteps approaching, Rowena turned and gave a dramatic curtsy as King Randolph entered the room. "Your Highness," she purred.

"Rowena," King Randolph greeted her. "Good of you to come on such short notice."

"Happy to be of service, dear cousin," she assured him. "It's good to be back in the castle."

"Come see my daughters," the king said, leading his cousin toward the throne room. "They're waiting for you."

As the king and his cousin entered the throne room, there was a line of princesses waiting to greet them. One by one, the king introduced his daughters.

Ashlyn, the eldest, stepped forward and curtsied. She was followed closely by Blair.

The king continued down the line, introducing Courtney, Delia, Edeline, and Fallon.

Fallon was far more interested in Rowena's monkey than in the duchess herself. "Is that a real monkey?" she asked excitedly. "Can I hold him?"

"No, don't touch him," Rowena ordered the girl. "He's quite rare. I bought him from a New World trader."

The king continued his introductions, pointing out the twins, Hadley and Isla, and the triplets, Janessa, Kathleen, and Lacey.

Then he stopped and counted the girls. There were only eleven. King Randolph sighed. "Let me guess," he said. "Genevieve is —"

"Right here," Genevieve called out as she dashed into the room with her pet kitten, Twyla, trotting at her heels. "Sorry, Papa." She turned and curtsied to Rowena. "It's nice to see you, Your Grace," she greeted her.

"Thank you, Genevieve," Rowena replied coldly. "Tell me, are you always late?"

Genevieve blushed slightly. "I guess, well, uh — yes. But I'm working on it."

Twyla stood at Genevieve's feet and stared curiously at Brutus. She had never seen a monkey before. Brutus stuck his tongue out at the kitten.

Rowena sighed and turned to the king. "You called me not a moment too soon," she told him. "You're absolutely right. Your girls are dreadful. . . ." She stopped, catching herself.

"Dreadful*ly* unprepared for royal life."

"I've . . . er . . . asked Duchess Rowena to take charge of your upbringing," the king explained to his daughters.

"But —" Genevieve began.

"No protests, please," her father stopped her. "You need to be proper princesses. Duchess Rowena will prepare you."

Rowena noted the shocked expressions on the girls' faces. "I have my work cut out for me," she huffed.

From that moment on, life changed. The princesses' days were no longer filled with reading, horseback riding, painting, and tennis. Now their hours were spent with Rowena. She taught them to use their beautiful silk fans to hide their faces, demonstrated which fork to use first at fancy dinner parties, and forced them to practice speaking with the same cold tone she herself used.

To make sure that all the princesses concentrated, the duchess took away their beautiful gowns and replaced them with drab dresses. She destroyed their beautiful canopy beds and gave each girl a plain cot with a wool blanket. She had Janessa's beloved insects taken away, and she smashed the tiny stool Lacey used to climb into bed.

In short, Rowena made life very unpleasant.

"She's so mean," Fallon grumbled as she lay on her lumpy cot one night.

"If Papa knew what Rowena was really like, he'd change his mind," Genevieve suggested.

"Talk to him, Genevieve," Blair pleaded.

As she curled up beneath her itchy blanket, Genevieve sighed. She would be glad to speak to her father. She only hoped he would listen.

"Now, where did we leave off?" King Randolph

20

asked Genevieve as they played a game of chess the following morning. "Bishop to queen three."

Genevieve enjoyed her chess matches with her father. Win or lose, the game seemed to bring them closer together. Which was exactly why Genevieve had chosen this time to tell her father what life with Rowena was *really* like.

"Papa, I was wondering," Genevieve began slowly as she moved her rook toward her father's bishop. "About Cousin Rowena . . ."

"Charming, isn't she?"

That wouldn't be the exact word Genevieve would have used to describe the duchess. Still, Genevieve sensed that she had to say something kind. "Very, uh, stylish," replied Genevieve. "But she's changing everything."

"As I've asked her to do," King Randolph told her.

"But we were fine before," Genevieve insisted.

"That's not what I heard, Genevieve. . . ."

Rowena's snobbish voice rang out suddenly.

Genevieve swiveled in her seat, and her eyes met Rowena's angry stare.

"But perhaps you're right," Rowena continued. "There's so much work to be done. What you really need is an entire team . . . tutors for protocol, diction, language, etiquette, style. It's exhausting just to think about. I should go."

"No, Rowena," the king assured her. "My girls need you. I can't embarrass them in front of the kingdom by bringing in groups of tutors."

"Well . . . if you really think I can be of service," Rowena purred.

"It's settled, then," King Randolph told Genevieve. "You must listen to the duchess. She knows what's best for you."

Genevieve did not miss the look of triumph that washed over Rowena's face. The princess leaped up and left the room in defeat.

"I hate to see her upset," King Randolph fretted.

"Girls are so emotional," Rowena told him. "What they need is proper guidance." She handed the king a cup of tea. "Here, my dear cousin, try this tea. Smooth and refreshing."

The king took the cup from her hand. Rowena raised hers in a toast. "To your . . . *health*," she murmured.

King Randolph sipped the tea as he stared at the doorway. His mind was on Genevieve.

Chapter 4
Queen Isabella's Gifts

One morning, just before dawn, while the triplets slept soundly, the older girls hurried to decorate their grim bedroom. They placed sweet-smelling wildflowers on three small chairs to make them look like thrones. Then the older girls began singing a beautiful song.

"Happy birthday, Janessa, Kathleen, and Lacey," Genevieve sang out, waking them gently.

As the triplets' eyes fluttered open, their

older sisters showered them with rose petals. Then, as the first rays of sunlight burst through the open window, the twelve princesses began a celebratory dance.

The girls were unaware that they were being watched by Brutus, Rowena's devious monkey. He ran off to alert his mistress to what was happening in the princesses' bedroom.

A few moments later, the duchess appeared in the doorway. "You're late," she scolded.

"Your Grace, we were celebrating a special birthday," Genevieve explained.

"That's no excuse," Rowena barked back angrily. "Until you learn etiquette, the celebrations will wait."

"But we always dance on our birthdays," Genevieve insisted. "Mother made it a family tradition."

"Sadly, your mother isn't here," Rowena reminded her coldly. "I am responsible for your upbringing. Dancing is now forbidden. And singing is out, too."

Rowena may have been able to forbid dancing, but she could not rid the girls of the magical memories their mother had left for them. That night, while the princesses prepared for bed, the triplets received special gifts from their sisters.

"When we turned five, Mother gave each of us a copy of her favorite story," Genevieve explained as the younger girls opened their gifts.

"She had one made for each daughter," Ashlyn added.

Lacey struggled to read the words on her book's cover. *"The . . . Dancing . . . Princess."*

Genevieve smiled proudly at her sister's effort. Then she gently took the book from her sister's hand and began to read the story. The younger girls were mesmerized by the tale of the beautiful princess who danced her way into a magical land.

"'The princess danced across the floor, stepping on each of the special stones,'" Genevieve read. "'Then, on the twelfth one, she twirled around three times, and to her amazement, a secret door opened.'"

"Where'd it go?" Janessa asked excitedly.

Genevieve read on, describing a place with trees of silver and gold, and flowers made of jewels. The girls' eyes opened wide as she read about the princess being able to dance and dance to her heart's content. The triplets sighed sadly as she explained that the magic land disappeared forever after the princess had danced there for three nights.

The triplets were tired by the time Genevieve finished reading the story. Lacey took her book and struggled to climb into her bed. But the book slipped from her hands and slid across the floor.

Genevieve bent to pick up the book, but stopped when she noticed something odd.

The flower on the cover matched a flower on the bedroom's stone floor.

Quickly, she took Kathleen's book and matched the flower on its cover to a different flower on the floor.

By now, all of the princesses were watching Genevieve. One by one, they grabbed their own books and began searching the stone floor.

"I found a match," Blair announced.

"Me, too," Courtney echoed. "What does it mean?"

"The story says the princess danced from stone to stone. . . ." Genevieve began. She leaped across the room, gracefully landing on each floral inlay. But when she reached the end of the floral path, nothing had happened.

"Maybe a different order?" she wondered aloud. "Oldest to youngest." She turned and leaped onto the stone that matched the flower on the cover of the eldest sister — Ashlyn's — book. A loud chiming noise came from beneath the floor. Next she leaped on the stone that matched Blair's book, and then Courtney's. Each time her foot landed on a stone, another musical note rang out.

Genevieve's heart was pounding with excitement as she reached the final stone —

the one that matched the flower on the cover of Lacey's book.

Strangely, nothing happened — not even the sound of a chime ringing.

"Why didn't mine work?" Lacey wondered.

Genevieve thought for a moment. "I forgot something," she recalled. "The princess twirled three times," she said, quoting the book as she spun around. "And on the third twirl . . ."

Just then, the stone floor shifted to the side, revealing a set of stairs. A bright light shone from below the floor, beckoning the girls to follow the stairs to a magical place.

Chapter 5
The Island of Silver and Gold

Genevieve bravely started down the stairs. Her kitten, Twyla, traveled close behind. One by one, the princesses followed, each passing through the magical light and into another world.

"Pinch me, I'm dreaming," Ashlyn gasped as she looked out at the glimmering lake before them.

"I'm having the same dream," Blair whispered, staring at the golden boat that stood at the dock, waiting to carry the

princesses across the water to a small island. In the center of the island was a beautiful golden pavilion, surrounded by jeweled flowers and silver and gold trees. Quickly, they boarded the boat and sailed across the lake. In a flash, they were standing in the middle of the pavilion.

Genevieve spun around excitedly on the elegant dance floor. "Come on, Lacey, dance with me," she said, grabbing her younger sister and twirling her.

Lacey giggled.

"I wish we had some music," Genevieve murmured.

No sooner had the words left her mouth than the petals of one of the jeweled flowers opened and sprinkled magical dust on the silent musical instruments that were lying nearby. Suddenly, the instruments came to life and began to play a lively tune. Genevieve's wish had been granted.

The music was irresistible. The sisters began to dance, twirling, leaping, and skipping across the floor of the pavilion. The

sense of freedom and joy they felt was clear from the beaming smiles on their faces.

Little Lacey struggled to keep up with the others. But she couldn't turn as quickly. She fell to the ground, scraping her knee. Tears filled the five-year-old's eyes.

Genevieve raced to her rescue. "I thought you were dancing beautifully," she assured her sister as she led her toward the lake and rubbed a bit of cool water on Lacey's knee. The water sparkled magically and the scrape instantly healed.

Lacey was amazed. As Genevieve returned to the dance floor, the smallest sister cupped her hands and gathered up some of the enchanted water. "I could use this all the time," she said to herself.

The dancing continued through the night, until finally the triplets grew weary. They sat down on a golden bench and fell fast asleep.

"It must be late," Genevieve said, waking the triplets. She looked down at the new dancing slippers Derek had made for her. "I actually wore out my shoes."

"It's a sign, you know," Ashlyn told her.

"Of what?" Genevieve asked.

"That we've danced enough for one night," Ashlyn replied. "We'd better go home before Rowena finds out we're gone."

The next morning, Rowena found herself in charge of twelve very tired princesses. "What exactly were you twelve doing last

night?" she demanded of them.

The girls all looked at one another, unsure of what to say. But before anyone could utter a response, the royal butler appeared at the door. "A visitor for the royal duchess," he announced. "A Mr. Fabian is here."

Rowena smiled slightly. "Oh, yes," she said as she hurried out of the room. "I was expecting him."

As Rowena scurried from the room, the butler delivered a second message. "The king requests his daughters visit him in his quarters."

Janessa leaped up excitedly. "Let's go tell Papa about last night!" she squealed as she dashed to her father's room.

Chapter 6
A Mystery Unfolds

"Well, look who's here," King Randolph exclaimed, sitting up in bed when his daughters entered the room. "The wild bunch."

Genevieve looked at him with concern. It was unusual for her father to still be in bed at this hour. "Are you sick?" she asked.

"Just tired," the king assured her. He turned to the triplets. "We were supposed to celebrate your birthday and I fell asleep. Is it too late to give you your presents?"

"No!" the three girls shouted at once.

The king reached over to his nightstand and picked up three small, round boxes. He handed one to each girl. Each box contained a small locket. The triplets were thrilled.

But Genevieve was not nearly as happy. As she glanced out the window, she spotted Rowena near the servants' entrance. The duchess was handing a small bundle to an oily-looking man in a blue coat.

Something awful was definitely going on. Genevieve could sense it.

Genevieve had no idea just how right she was. As Rowena returned to the castle, Brutus greeted her in the throne room. He dangled a single worn dancing shoe in front of Rowena's eyes.

Rowena studied the shoe carefully. "Worn through. Those spoiled brats were out dancing with princes." She gasped slightly as she realized what that could mean. "If princes fall for those pampered pretties, my plans are ruined."

Just then, Rowena heard singing coming from the king's room. "What are they up to?" she said angrily. Grabbing a tray of tea, she raced over to the king's bedchamber.

"I thought you had a headache," Rowena said, bursting into the room unannounced.

"I do, but I love when they sing for me," the king explained.

Rowena shook her head. "Look how pale you are, dear cousin," she clucked, pouring a cup of tea for him. She turned to the princesses. "Enough for now, girls. Out."

"Papa, maybe you should call for the doctor," Genevieve suggested. Rowena glanced sharply at Genevieve but said nothing.

An hour later, the royal doctor appeared at the king's bedside. He examined him from head to toe and then proclaimed, "Your Highness, if you continue to rest and take this elixir, I believe you will recover shortly."

"That's good news," the king said.

Rowena took the medicine from the doctor. "Allow me," she said sweetly.

"Twice daily should do the trick," the doctor instructed her as he took his leave.

Rowena followed the doctor out of the king's chamber. She waited for him to leave the castle and then, with an evil smile on her face, poured the medicine into a potted plant.

As Rowena pretended to care for the king, the princesses were in the front garden of the castle. They circled eagerly around Derek, who had just arrived with a fresh trunk of shoes.

"I've brought the new shoes, as you requested," the handsome cobbler told the princesses. "Were the ones before not to your liking?"

"Not at all," Ashlyn assured him. "We just wore them out."

"We've been dancing," Genevieve explained, stepping on twelve imaginary stones and then twirling three times, just as she had the night before. "A magical time," she sighed.

Ashlyn walked over and handed Derek her well-worn pair of shoes. "Can you fix them?" she asked.

Derek examined the shoes carefully. "Is that gold dust?" he asked.

"It's a secret." Genevieve gave him a teasing smile.

"Oh, of course," Derek said quickly, obviously feeling quite flustered. "I didn't mean to pry." He handed Genevieve a new pair of shoes. "I hope these last longer," he added. Then he turned and walked off.

Genevieve raced after him. "I didn't think you were prying," she assured the cobbler as she caught up to him. She stopped for a moment. "Derek, may I ask you a favor?"

"Me, Your Highness?" Derek asked.

Genevieve nodded. "Earlier, I saw Duchess Rowena give something to a man. A Mr. Fabian. Would you find out who he is?"

Derek nodded. He would never refuse anything Princess Genevieve asked of him.

Chapter 7
A Secret Revealed

Rowena was taking no more chances. As the girls retired to their bedroom that night, she ordered her manservant, Desmond, to stand sentry at their door all night long.

But, of course, the princesses would not be leaving their room through the door. The moment they were sure Rowena was gone for the evening, Genevieve danced across the floor until the stone tile shifted, and the magical staircase reappeared. Then the girls hurried down the stairs, boarded the golden boat, and traveled across the lake to the magical dancing pavilion.

Ashlyn glanced at a jeweled flower that hung on a trellis. "I wish we had ballet music," she said.

Instantly, the flower's petals opened, releasing magical dust. Suddenly, the majestic sounds of an orchestra filled the room.

As usual, Genevieve was the first to dance. Her sisters soon joined her, happy to be far from Rowena. Here, at least, the princesses were free.

As the princesses danced the night away, Derek and his bird, Felix, traveled the

kingdom in a horse-drawn cart, in search of Mr. Fabian. They finally spotted him on a dirt road far from the castle.

But as soon as Mr. Fabian spotted Derek, he kicked his horse hard and galloped away. Luckily, Derek's horse was equally fast. After a few moments, the cobbler was able to pass Mr. Fabian and force him to stop.

"I have been asked to inquire about your business with the duchess," Derek told Mr. Fabian.

"That's between me and the duchess, isn't it?" Mr. Fabian retorted.

"I wouldn't want to get my master angry," Felix warned. "The last time somebody refused him, the fool was never heard from again."

"Felix, that's not true," Derek scolded the bird.

Felix shrugged. "Derek, you're quite right.

They did manage to find one of his shoes."

Of course, Felix was making that all up. But Mr. Fabian didn't know it. "I'm just a simple apothecary," he insisted nervously. "I sell herbs and remedies."

"What did you sell the duchess?" Derek asked suspiciously.

"I almost didn't sell her anything. She doesn't pay her bills." Mr. Fabian lifted a small satchel from his bag. "This time she came through." He unwrapped the package and revealed an ornate silver goblet.

Derek raised his lantern to get a better look at the goblet. "'Queen Isabella,'" he gasped, reading the inscription. Princess Genevieve would be heartbroken to know that one of her mother's precious possessions was in the hands of this slimy man. "I'll buy it," Derek declared.

"That's a laugh!" Felix cawed. "What do

we have that's worth as much as a silver goblet?"

"A talking bird might do it," Mr. Fabian suggested.

Derek tilted his head slightly and considered the suggestion. Felix looked at him nervously. Lucky for the bird, Derek was only kidding. Instead, he traded the man his horse and cart for the silver goblet. As Mr. Fabian rode off, the cobbler began walking down the dirt road.

"Where are we going?" Felix asked.

Derek pointed to the goblet. "To show Princess Genevieve this."

"That'll take us forever," Felix groaned.

Derek rolled his eyes. "Don't make me wish I kept the horse and cart instead of you."

Felix didn't say another word for the rest of the journey.

Chapter 8
A Difficult Decision

The next morning, Rowena was quite pleased with herself. Everything seemed to be going her way. The king was growing weaker by the hour, and Desmond had assured her that the princesses had been in their beds all night.

But when she opened the door to the princesses' bedroom, she found all twelve still fast asleep in their beds. Worse than that, she found twelve pairs of worn dancing shoes.

"Everybody line up!" the duchess shouted

angrily. "This instant. Move! Move!"

The girls leaped up from their beds and, although they were only half awake, managed to line up before the duchess.

"Where were you dancing last night?" Rowena demanded. She pointed to Edeline. "Answer me, Delia."

"I'm Edeline," the frightened princess replied.

"I don't care," Rowena bellowed. "Answer me."

"We . . . uh . . . danced at a pavilion."

Rowena wheeled around and glared at Kathleen. "How did you get there?" she demanded.

"The magic boat took us," Kathleen replied fearfully.

"Please." Rowena rolled her eyes scornfully. She turned to Lacey. "You're the runt of the family," she roared at her. "Tell me

the truth or you'll all pay."

Genevieve leaped in front of her young sister. "How can you talk to her that way?" she demanded bravely.

Rowena scoffed. "How dare *you* talk back to *me*?" she growled. "You're no better than common maids. Maybe if I treat you like maids, you'll change your minds about lying to me. This morning you shall clean the front garden. I want it spotless."

"But —" Genevieve began.

"Tsk-tsk," Rowena interrupted. "Talking back? Now you'll scrub the steps as well."

It took the princesses all day to scrub the steps and clean the garden. By nightfall they were so tired they could barely stand. But that didn't stop Rowena from demanding even more of the girls.

"Tired? Sore? Frustrated?" she taunted as she burst into their bedchamber. "Maybe now I'll hear some truth."

"We told you the truth," Genevieve insisted.

"Apparently you didn't learn your lesson," Rowena said. "Tomorrow you'll clean the stables. As for tonight . . ." She lifted a large key from her pocket. "I'm locking you in. Nobody is going dancing. I promise you that."

The princesses stared at her in surprise.

"Papa would never lock us in," Delia said.

"Your father is sick," Rowena informed her. "And who can blame him? Taking care of you with your wild ways. If you really want your father to get better, you'll leave him alone. The truth is, you embarrass him. Why do you think he brought me here?"

As Rowena swept out of their room, the girls looked at one another.

"I never knew Papa was so disappointed in us," Courtney remarked.

"Everything's so wrong here," Fallon moaned sadly.

Twyla, looking up at Genevieve's sad face, leaped up on her fuzzy back paws. She tried to dance, hoping it would cheer the princess.

"Twyla has the right idea," Genevieve told her sisters. "There's still one place we can go where we won't disappoint anyone."

"If Papa thinks we're a burden . . ." Hadley began.

"He can get better if we're not around," Isla concluded.

"Maybe it's best if we go," Ashlyn agreed.

One by one, the princesses began to gather their dancing shoes. They would have to leave. It was the only way to save their father.

Chapter 9
The Secret Is Out!

Early the next morning, Rowena arrived at the princesses' bedchamber bright and early. As she arrived, Desmond bowed low. "Nobody came or left, my lady," he assured her.

Rowena unlocked the door and prepared to wake the girls. Much to her surprise, they were gone. "Desmond, get in here!" she shouted angrily.

The servant looked around the empty room with amazement. "But I never left the door," he swore.

"Are you telling me they just vanished into thin air?" Rowena demanded. "Find them!"

As Desmond went off in search of the princesses, Rowena headed into the king's bedchamber. The girls might be missing, but that didn't mean she would abandon the rest of her plan.

"Feeling any better today?" she asked, pretending to care.

"I'm afraid not," the king moaned. "I'm so tired. I can barely keep my eyes open. How are the girls? Perhaps they'll have time to visit me today."

Rowena didn't answer. Instead, she poured him a cup of tea. As the king wearily closed his eyes, Rowena pulled a dark bottle from beneath her sleeve and slipped several drops of poison into the cup.

"You take good care of me, Rowena," the king murmured.

"It's true," Rowena replied, choking back a laugh. "Nobody treats you the way I do."

As the king drank his poisoned tea, Rowena scurried out of the room. She had to make sure that those girls were found immediately. There was too much at stake.

Later that afternoon, Derek the cobbler arrived at the castle gate. "Hello, sir," he said as the butler opened the door. "May I see Princess Genevieve?"

The royal butler looked in both directions, making sure there was no one around who might overhear them. "The princesses are missing," he whispered to Derek. "I heard Duchess Rowena say they've run away."

Suddenly, Rowena's servant appeared. "Cobbler, we don't need you today," he said angrily, slamming the door in Derek's face.

Derek stepped back from the doorway.

"Tell me you're going to leave," Felix begged. He definitely didn't want to disobey someone as scary as Rowena.

"Eventually," Derek assured the bird as he walked around the side of the castle and began climbing up the flowering vines that led to the balcony outside the princesses' chamber.

"You're crazy!" Felix cawed. "If you're caught, you'll be thrown in the dungeon."

But Derek would not be put off by threats. He entered the princesses' chamber. The twelve beds were still made. Obviously, no one had slept in that room all night.

That was odd. But even stranger was the fact that there was shoe oil on the twelve floral stones on the floor. Quickly, Derek raced over to the first stone and stepped on the floral inlay. He heard a bell chime. Then another chime rang out as he stepped on the second stone. By the third chime, Derek remembered something.

"Her dance," he murmured, as he began imitating the dance Genevieve had done in the garden. "Seven, eight, nine, ten, eleven. . . ." He looked down. "This is it. The last one."

"Now what?" Felix wondered.

"Turn three times," Derek answered.

"You've got be kidding." Felix laughed as the cobbler twirled around. "What do you think will happen? The floor will open up?"

Just then, the secret stairway came into view.

"Anything else to add?" Derek asked as he began walking down the stairs.

For once, Felix was speechless. He flew down the stairs behind his master.

But as Derek and Felix disappeared into the floor, they were unaware that their entire dance had been seen by the peering eyes of Rowena's monkey, Brutus. And he was only too willing to hurry and show his mistress what he had seen.

"This is what you wanted to show me?" Rowena bellowed a few moments later as she watched her monkey leap from stone to stone on the princesses' floor. "What on earth are you doing?"

Brutus hopped onto the twelfth stone and waited. But nothing happened.

"I am wasting my time," Rowena sighed. But before she could turn and leave, Brutus finished imitating the dance he had seen Derek do. Twirling three times on his little heels, he stood back as the stone floor moved to the side, and the staircase came into view.

Rowena's eyes opened wide. So that was how the girls had disappeared! She smiled slightly as she descended the stairs. A moment later, she stood by the golden lake, staring at the pavilion across the way.

"I wish I could see what was going on," she murmured. A moment later, one of the jeweled flowers opened its petal. Magical dust flew up in the air, and a spyglass appeared in Rowena's hands.

"Will wonders never cease?" the duchess cooed, surprised by the flower's magic. "Get me some of those flowers," she commanded as she peered through the spyglass at the twelve princesses. Brutus did as he was told, pulling two flowers from the ground.

"Hurry," Rowena ordered with a sly grin. "Opportunity knocks."

Derek was unaware that anyone had followed him to the magical land. His only concern at the moment was how to get across the lake and warn Princess Genevieve that the duchess could not be trusted.

His eyes landed on a small rowboat. In a flash, he boarded the boat and rowed his way across the lake.

Princess Genevieve could not believe her eyes as he approached the pavilion a few moments later. "Derek!?" she exclaimed, surprised. "What are you doing here?"

Derek pulled the silver goblet from his cloak. "You were right not to trust the duchess. She gave this to the stranger you saw."

"He gave up his horse and carriage to get you that," Felix told her.

"It belongs with you, not him," Derek explained shyly.

Genevieve smiled at him, and a glimmer of hope flashed across her face. Could it be that Derek liked her as much as she liked him?

"Why would Rowena steal Mother's goblet?" asked Ashlyn.

But there was no time for any questions. "We have to go home and tell Papa," Genevieve told her sisters. She paused and looked around sadly, realizing the consequences of what she had just said. "But if we leave now, we can never come back."

Her sisters looked at her, confused.

"Mother's story," Genevieve reminded them. "The princess visited the land only three times before it vanished forever."

"I can't imagine never coming back," Blair murmured.

"Rowena may not think we're proper

princesses, but we are princesses just the same," Genevieve insisted. "We can't turn our backs when things get difficult. Papa needs us."

Quickly, the sisters followed Genevieve out to the lake. But as they prepared to board the golden boat, it began to disappear into thin air. A moment later, the boathouse disappeared, then the stairs, and finally the glowing doorway itself.

"We're trapped," Edeline gasped.

"What are we going to do?" Blair wondered.

Chapter 10
The Escape!

There was only one person horrible enough to want to trap the princesses. Rowena, of course, was behind it all. She and Desmond had smashed the magical stones in the princesses' bedroom, destroying the passage back. Now that the girls were gone, there was only one thing left for Rowena to do — finish off King Randolph. Then the kingdom would be hers!

As a chilly wind blew, she headed into the king's chamber. "Your attention is sorely needed on affairs of the kingdom," she told King Randolph, knowing full well he was too weak to handle anything.

The king sighed. "I know this is a tremendous burden," he told Rowena, "but would you ever consider standing in for me — just until I recover?"

Rowena smirked to herself. *Recover?* She would never let that happen. But she smiled at the king. "I would do anything to assist you," she assured him.

King Randolph motioned to one of his secretaries, who pulled out a piece of parchment and a pen.

"I, King Randolph, hereby proclaim Duchess Rowena the queen, until I can resume my royal duties," the king dictated.

"I am honored," Rowena said, taking her new crown from a nearby satin pillow and placing it squarely on her head. She smiled triumphantly. With the king nearing death, and the princesses trapped in their magical prison, there was no one to stop her now.

But Rowena had misjudged the princesses. They were not the type to give up — particularly when the safety of their father was in jeopardy. At that very moment, they were searching for a way out of the magical kingdom.

It was Genevieve who developed a plan. "I wish to know a way out," she said, turning to the jeweled flowers. At that very moment, several of the jeweled flowers bloomed, and magic dust sprinkled onto twelve stones on the pavilion floor. The pathway became clear.

"We danced our way in. . . ." Hadley began.

"We can dance our way out," Isla said, finishing her twin's thought.

Genevieve started for the first glowing stone. Derek's foot touched the stone at the same moment. Instantly, the stone chimed.

Derek smiled warmly and held out his hand to the princess. "May I have this dance?" he asked, sounding bolder than he ever had before.

"My pleasure," Genevieve replied, taking his arm.

The princess and the cobbler waltzed over the stones, making sure their feet touched on each stone at the exact same time. As they reached the twelfth and final stone, a circular staircase magically appeared. They had found their way home.

And Genevieve had found her true love.

One by one, the twelve dancing princesses climbed the magical staircase and before long found themselves back on the castle grounds. As soon as the last princess stepped off the last stair, the stairway disappeared, closing off the magical land forever.

"I'll miss it," Ashlyn sighed.

"We all will," Fallon agreed.

"Let's go home," Genevieve urged. She was anxious to tell her father about Rowena's evil plan.

But Rowena had been prepared for the possibility of the princesses returning. As they passed by a large hedge, the girls and Derek overheard two sentries speaking.

"Queen Rowena has given us orders," one sentry told the other. "We must capture the princesses and throw them in the dungeon."

The girls stared at one another in amazement. *Queen* Rowena?

"And the king?" the second sentry wondered.

"He's very ill and won't last the night," his partner replied.

"We have to save him!" Genevieve whispered to her sisters.

"But if Rowena is queen . . ." Courtney began fearfully.

Genevieve shook her head. "We have something Rowena doesn't," she said firmly. "The power of twelve. I have a plan."

Chapter 11
Wishes Granted

Knowing there was no time to waste, Genevieve immediately put her plan into action. Since Blair was the best horsewoman, she was given the task of taking one of the sentry's horses and riding off in search of the doctor.

The other sisters were placed in charge of leading the palace sentries on a wild goose chase, so Genevieve would be able to sneak into the castle and warn their father. She could only hope she would get there in time.

Unfortunately, just as Genevieve and Derek entered the king's room, she saw her father fall, and an empty teacup crash to the floor. "Papa!" the princess shouted, rushing into the room. She turned to Rowena. "What did you do to him?"

The new queen was not about to put up with any arguments with the princess. Rowena took from her pocket one of the jeweled flowers she had stolen from the pavilion. She then turned to a suit of armor in the corner of the room and declared, "I wish for armor to protect the queen."

Instantly, two suits of armor came to life.

One wielded a mace, while the other held a sword. When the first suit raised its mace, Derek quickly dove out of the way. Instead, the mace struck a desk and broke it into pieces.

Now the other suit of armor turned on Genevieve. When Derek saw that she was in danger, he pushed a table between her and the armor. Genevieve dove under the table just in time. This table also fell into pieces, but Genevieve was not harmed.

Quickly, Genevieve handed a broken table leg to Derek. He swung it hard, knocking the mace from the first suit of armor.

Genevieve grabbed the fallen mace. She swiftly wrapped it around the legs of the other suit of armor. The armor fell to the floor with a mighty crash and shattered into pieces.

"Nice to have a partner," Genevieve told Derek.

"More than nice," Derek agreed.

The armor had been destroyed, but Rowena still had one more flower in her hand. "The dungeon's too good for you," the duchess told Genevieve. "So why not give you what you've always wanted? I wish you would dance forever and ever and ever."

As the jeweled flower bloomed, Rowena blew hard, to make sure the magic dust fell on Genevieve. But Genevieve was ready for her. She pulled a dainty fan from her dress and began waving it, just as Rowena had taught her in etiquette class. The magic dust blew back in Rowena's direction.

Suddenly, Rowena's shoes began to glow. Her foot started tapping wildly.

"I'll help you, Your Grace!" Desmond shouted. But as he rushed to her aid, some of the dust landed on his shoes. The duchess and

her servant were joined together, destined to be dancing partners for the rest of their lives.

As Rowena and Desmond danced off the castle grounds, Derek and Genevieve turned their attention to the ailing king.

"He's barely breathing," Derek said, placing a hand on the king's pulse.

"What if it's too late?" Genevieve asked nervously. "Where is Blair with the doctor?"

Suddenly, a small voice came from the far corner of the room. "I think I can help him,"

Lacey said, pulling a small vial from around her neck. She poured a few drops of clear water onto her father's lips. "It's from the lake," she explained. "I took some after I scraped my knee."

Suddenly, King Randolph's eyes fluttered open. Color returned to his face. "Lacey?" he asked, looking into the eyes of his youngest daughter. He glanced up. "Genevieve?"

"We thought we'd lost you," Genevieve said, hugging him hard.

"It was Rowena, poisoning me," the king deduced. "How could I have been so blind?" He looked at his daughters. "I let you down when I started to care what others said. You are each special, beautiful princesses, and you'll do great things in your own way — as your mother always told me!"

Chapter 12
A Royal Wedding

Genevieve walked gracefully across the beautifully manicured castle lawn, her long white train flowing behind her as she moved. Everyone present gasped at her grace as she glided toward her groom. Genevieve was, without a doubt, the most beautiful bride anyone in the kingdom had ever seen.

Derek stepped up to greet her and, taking her hand in his, led her to the white gazebo, which had been decorated with the most lovely flowers in the kingdom. The bride and groom stood there for a moment, professing their love for each other. And then, after being pronounced husband and wife, Derek took Genevieve in his arms. And when the music started to play, they began to dance. Now, and for always, they would be in perfect step.